Enjoy a sneak preview of
Silhouette Nocturne books

Desire Calls
by Caridad Piñeiro

Mere mortals and lesser vampires feared her powers as an elder. But when she is reunited with a vampire who possesses the spirit she has found lacking in men for nearly two thousand years, the elder knows she's met her match. For he is a man who makes her question whether she should let go of the last vestige of humanity that has created such disquiet within her, or risk everything to embrace the love she's denied for centuries.

Death Calls
by Caridad Piñeiro

When an FBI agent falls in love with a vampire, she discovers that darkness calls to humans as well as vampires. But her vampire lover fears losing her and the void that will fill him without her. It's not until a case draws her into a purely human darkness that her lover must make a decision: Can he let her go? Or will he step between her and death, no matter if she hates him afterward?

Eternally
by Maureen Child

He was a Guardian. An immortal fighter of evil. For centuries he'd heard the legend of Destined Mates…but he never believed it until now. Joining with the woman he'd sworn to protect would make him strong enough to defeat any demon from hell. But the cost might be losing the woman who was his true salvation.

CONTENTS

DESIRE CALLS
CARIDAD PIÑEIRO

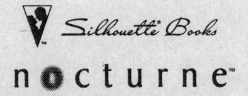

Silhouette Books

n⚫cturne™

Chapter 1

The piazza always provided a fine selection for dining, Stacia thought as she sat on the railing along the edge of the Bernini fountain in Rome's Piazza Navona. She gazed at the choices available in various spots around the square. French. German. Italian, of course.

Her stomach rumbled with hunger. It had been a day since she had eaten. Placing a hand over her belly, she rose and sashayed toward her first pick, but as she neared the Frenchman, she realized he was beyond loaded. The stench of cheap wine clung to his shirt and oozed from his pores.

Shaking her head, she thought of the oft-repeated adage all those television chefs used: If it's not good enough to drink, it's not good enough for cooking. Or in her case, for eating. That cheap stuff just left a bad aftertaste in her mouth along with a wickedly nasty buzz.

She preferred something cleaner on her palate tonight.

Which definitely had her bypassing the Aryan god she had noticed just a short distance away from the Frenchman. Germans were always a trifle heavy in her belly. However, the broad set of his shoulders and well-muscled chest made her reconsider. She loved her men big and strong and so she lingered by the front of the outdoor café where he was seated. Even made eye contact with him for a moment.

Amazing crystal-blue eyes twinkled with interest. That much was clear.

Stacia smiled back, thinking that maybe he might be worth a nibble after all. Maybe they might actually even click, finally providing her with true pleasure after nearly two thousand years of undead life.

Mr. Tall, Blond and Brawny rose from his chair, seemingly intent on making a move in her direction, but suddenly an equally tall, blond and muscled woman joined him. Seeing that his attention was on Stacia, his companion began a harangue loud enough to make heads turn. The man plopped down into his chair, looking like a dog with its tail tucked between his legs.

No spirit. That was so not good, Stacia thought and moved onward, still in search of something to satisfy her hunger.

She needed a man who could not only take a lickin', but gave as good as he got. And not just when he was in a fight. It had been a good long while since any man had really satisfied her in bed, one of the downsides of having lived so long. Of being a vampire elder.

Even her own kind avoided her at times, aware that with her age came vast power, but also vast hunger. For blood. For sex. For control over lesser vamps. She didn't want to admit that in her case, she still hungered for love. For real passion and desire.

Things she hadn't felt in way too long.

Some of the other elders said that she was foolish to yearn for such things. That she should let go of the last little bit of humanity within her that prompted such desires. Then, and only then, could she truly relish the immense vampire power that her age provided.

Stubbornly, though, Stacia refused to relinquish that lingering trace of humanity. Of want for something more than an eternal existence filled with only….

A fine-looking American caught her eye as he laughed at the antics of his rowdy friends in front of one bar. He was as big and blond as the whipped Aryan she had bypassed earlier, but as his gaze met hers, she saw steel there. Luscious gray eyes were framed by a sheath of shaggy, sunbleached hair.

Stacia circled Mr. Surfer Dude, making eye contact and clearly letting the young man know that this might just be his lucky night.

It worked without her using even a bit of her vampire

power. A flirtatious smile and her feminine wiles had been enough.

He approached, leaned down from his greater height and in awfully accented Italian, asked, *"Parla Inglese?"*

"Do we need to talk?" she said with a sexy wink and inclined her head in the direction of a nearby alley.

The young man smiled broadly and after a quick glance back at his friends, who hooted and carried on at his "score," he took hold of her hand and followed her.

Stacia led him farther back into the narrow alley, although not so far that he would think anything was amiss. Just far enough that he would believe a strong shout could still be heard out in the piazza. Not that she would give him the opportunity to call out.

Toward the middle of the alley, the night closed in around them, with only the dimmest light from the full moon above. Clothed in darkness, the young man surprised her by becoming the aggressor, grabbing her forcefully and pinning her to the jagged brick wall.

"Like it rough, do you?" she said, but he didn't answer since with quick hands he had already undone the laces on her leather vest and was gazing down at her breasts as they spilled free.

When he bent to suck at them, she moaned, thinking that he was exceptionally gifted with his mouth. Between her legs, the throb of human desire rose up, aching for fulfillment.

She quickly undid his jeans, reached past the loose folds of denim to the boxer shorts below.

How she loved this new fashion that made it so easy to free him. To stroke the rather magnificent length of him.

He bit down on one nipple as she caressed him, dragging a gasp from her.

"Sorry," he mumbled, as he lifted the almost non-existent hem of her black leather miniskirt, cupped her bare buttocks and urged her upward.

With a surge, she jumped up and wrapped her legs around him, then drove down, crying out as the long thick length of him penetrated her. He was deliciously big, much like the rest of him.

His own groan was from the gut as she leaned back against the brick wall and he pounded into her, all finesse forgotten as he strove for release. He looked down and watched the play of his hips against hers, as if fascinated by that sight. His blond curls brushing the naked skin between her legs.

Stacia considered the emotions flitting across his face. Passion rose, dilating his eyes into shards of slate gray. Almost charcoal gray, she realized as he met her gaze before dipping his head down again to suck on her breasts.

Inside her, heat built. Desire awakened the demon that hungered for so much. She threw her head back, allowed the beast to slowly emerge so that it could experience it all. The dark of the night enveloped them in its secrecy. The strength of his youth brought her closer and closer to completion. The musky smells of their lovemaking pushed her over the edge.

She called out her physical completion and laid her

face against his. Bent her head and kissed the crook of his neck. His skin was damp. Salty. His blood surged, singing through his veins as his heart beat quickened while he strove for his own release.

Sweet, sweet blood. Pulsing beneath her lips.

In a heartbeat, she finally loosed her restraints on the beast. Her fangs burst forth and pierced the fragile skin of his neck.

He called out then in a strangled cry laced with pain, but also with the acknowledgment of passion like no other he had ever experienced—the passion borne from a vampire's kiss.

Blood spilled onto her lips from her fangs as she drank, experiencing the surge of strength and lust that came from feeding. His sweet young blood brought the rush of life to her undead body.

He tasted like the ocean and sun. Salty. So tasty that Stacia could have kept on going until she drained him dry, only he had done well by her tonight, satisfying one hunger while leaving another unfulfilled.

The young man's knees weakened from the loss of blood and Stacia hopped off him. With her greater vampire strength, she gently eased him down to the uneven pavement.

He was rather handsome, she thought, gazing down at him as he stared up at her, disoriented. The bite mark at his neck was already healing and come the morning, he would remember nothing. Feel no worse off than if he had a bad hangover, she thought as she quickly closed up her vest.

And she would feel—

Still alone, she thought, hurrying from the alley as if by doing so, she could escape the bleakness of her existence.

Once out in the piazza, she realized that it was time to move on. She would not find satisfaction here.

As she strolled through the square, it occurred to her New York would be good this time of year. Lots of fine dining there and the wannabes at the Blood Bank were always good for a laugh.

Imagine, wanting to be human again, she thought. What good was that? she asked herself, ignoring the little voice in her head which reminded her that with humanity came—

Love.

Chapter 2

The Lair was hopping as it always was on a Saturday night. Not that Blake was a regular at that club, preferring the Blood Bank with its edgier clientele and higher volume of vampires. The people here—not even serious vamp poseurs—were just interested in a flirtation with the dark side, like visiting an Undead Disneyland.

They loved the look of the place, from the faux stone walls to the hundreds of realistic bat bodies clinging to the ceiling above which created the illusion that you were in an underground cavern. Even the bar fed into the macabre fantasy: the sign for The Lair seemed to drip blood from its letters onto the bar's gleaming stainless-steel surface.

Blake chuckled at the crowd, thinking that they

paled in comparison to those true believers at the Blood Bank. Where a bloke could be guaranteed a nice shot of blood or a nip at a willing neck.

His friend Ryder, the owner of this club, had no blood of any kind on the drink menu. Not even some hearty beef blood. Worse yet, he had a strict No Bite policy for the real vampires who occasionally dropped by.

A shame, Blake thought, as one rather attractive young woman bumped into him and smiled, sending the clear signal that she was interested in his rather fine punk self. He ignored her, glancing through the murky light to the luminous steel counter of the bar, where his former love labored, either unaware of his presence or ignoring him.

He suspected it was the latter since as her sire, they were irrevocably connected. But that didn't mean they were meant to be together he had realized some months ago.

Blond, green-eyed and beautiful, Meghan stood behind the counter, smiling as she poured drinks and took money.

Blake remembered that smile well. Recalled the night they had met at the Blood Bank, where Meghan had gone on a dare with a group of her coed friends. Even done up in her version of Goth, with black denim clinging to every luscious curve of her youthful body, her brightness had shone through.

She had clearly been intrigued by his swagger and Cockney accent. They had gone off alone, just to talk at first because after over a century of life, it wasn't all that easy to find someone to connect with. Bullocks, they had definitely connected, he recalled.

She had made him laugh. Made him remember just how wonderful spending time with someone could be. That hadn't happened in...forever.

When Meghan had agreed to go with him to one of the back rooms at the Blood Bank, he hadn't intended to sire her. He had just wanted to savor her sexy All-American looks, lithe body and the promise in her forest green eyes. Revel in the way her sexiness was laced with humor and light after his long life in the dark.

But somewhere along the way, he had lost control.

The wonderfully sexy and too human interlude had awakened a longing he hadn't acknowledged for some time. When he released the demon, he told himself it was just to take a nibble of all her goodness. To just savor a little longer the lovemaking that had been so ful-filling, so alive with light and passion and just sheer fun.

Her skin had been soft against his lips as he bit down on her neck. Her scent, so fresh and clean, had obliter-ated the earthier odor of the blood. And her body...

She had screamed out at his possession, but not just with pain. When she clutched him to her, he realized that he hadn't wanted it to end. Ever.

Blake had nearly sucked her dry. By the time the extent of his feeding registered, he had been left with a painful choice. Let her die or sire her. He had taken too much blood for her to survive.

So Blake had turned her, earning her hatred as Meghan fought the reality of her new existence. In the past year, he had redeemed himself by saving her life and that of her guardian, but things would never be right between them. Which was why he lurked in the shadows, wishing that he would find someone else who could bring light and love to his life. Someone else to connect with again since his chance encounter with Meghan had shown him that love was still possible for someone like him.

You're a pitiful bloke, he told himself, straightening and pulling his black leather jacket closed. It was time he moved on and found another young thing to satisfy him. He couldn't spend the rest of his life worrying about the little chit who would be forever twenty-one thanks to his actions.

Most women would be pleased by that possibility, vain creatures that they were.

Turning on his heel, he left The Lair in a burst of vampire speed, exiting out onto the streets of Tribeca. Leaping up the landings of a nearby fire escape until he was on the rooftop of an adjacent building.

The moon was full, bathing New York City in silvery light. A nip lingered in the early spring air, not that it bothered his vampire thermostat. But he was a mite peckish and needed a bite of something to ease that hunger.

He leaped from one rooftop to the next until he arrived at the familiar alley before the Blood Bank.

Blake slipped down from the roof, landing noiselessly on the cobblestones. He sauntered to the door and flashed some fang at the bouncer who let him in past the long line of people waiting to enter.

Inside, it was as dim as The Lair, but without all the theatrical touches. Worn chairs and tables bore the scars of the violence for which the Blood Bank was known in the undead world. Opening his vampire senses, he recognized the hum of power that said there were others of his kind here. But more importantly, he detected the commanding vibrations from an elder. A very familiar elder, he thought and glanced toward the bar.

Stacia in all her glory.

The night had finally taken a turn for the better, Blake thought and walked toward the bar.

Chapter 3

With a rather bored sigh, Stacia placed the glass filled with blood from a nouveau yuppie fresh from Chelsea on the gouged counter before her. She had been hoping to run into some familiar faces, but other than Foley, the owner of the bar, the night had been quiet, until...

She swiveled on her stool as she sensed a familiar vamp energy and took note of him as he approached.

Blake. In his best Billy Idol get-up. His chain-studded jeans tight against lean hips, black leather jacket strained against his broad shoulders. Playfully spiked blond hair revealed a face with marvelous bone structure.

As he realized he had her attention, the swagger in his step increased. A broad smile spread across his face and swept up into his deep blue eyes.

Stacia found herself smiling back, even if it was just Blake.

When he stood before her, he placed his hands on his hips, drawing aside the jacket to reveal a black T-shirt that clung lovingly to his muscles. "Blimey, luv. It's been too long since you've visited."

"Been missing me? That's a surprise," she said and with a wave of her hand, signaled for the bartender to bring Blake a drink.

"Why would that be a surprise, luv?" He slipped onto the open stool beside her. When the bartender placed a glass with blood before him, he raised it and offered up a toast. "To *old*— We're definitely old, but are we *friends?*"

Stacia laughed harshly and picked up her glass, but didn't return the toast. Eyeing him over the rim of the glass, she said, "A gentleman wouldn't mention a lady's age and as for being friends... Why aren't you afraid of me?"

Blake, ever confident and even more playful, leaned toward her and whispered close to her lips, "Should I be?"

Picking up her hand, she inclined her head toward the direction of the vampire bartender and made believe she was squeezing. The bartender suddenly dropped the glass he held and grabbed at his throat, fighting for air.

"Should you be afraid?" she asked, almost hoping that Blake would prove her right and make a fast exit as so many of the vamps at the Blood Bank had done upon her arrival.

"A man's got to face his fears," Blake said calmly and sipped his blood, barely glancing in the direction of the barkeep whose sallow vampire skin was starting to turn slightly blue.

With a flick of her hand, Stacia released her hold on the vampire and examined Blake, sensing something different about him. Something a bit more...intriguing. He had changed since the last time she had seen him. "So you don't fear me..."

"Should I?" he asked again. "Do you have some nefarious plan for me, luv?" His voice was laced with humor and not a whit of the anxiety she usually inspired in other lesser vampires. When he gestured in the direction of the back rooms, she chuckled.

"Get real. Me and you? Do I look like I'm slumming?"

With a careless shrug, Blake slipped off the stool and with a nod said, "Well, then it's goodbye, I guess. "

Stacia controlled her surprise at his seeming nonchalance and watched him walk away, his swagger drawing the attention of quite a few female heads. Stupid human females who didn't realize that to Blake, they were just a possible snack.

When he actually sidled up to one, bent that peroxided head and said something to the young woman that had her laughing, annoyance flared through Stacia. She didn't know why. At best, she and Blake were long-time acquaintances. Not friends. Elders had few friends, not even other elders.

There were usually too many power plays going on to permit true friendships to develop.

Blake's attitude was therefore…refreshing.

As he and the young woman headed onto the dance floor and plastered their bodies against each other, Stacia decided that it was time she had some fun, as well, instead of just sitting there, moping.

Moping was so pitiful.

Scoping out the crowd in the bar, she noticed one young man seated at a booth along the far wall. Big and powerful. The black T-shirt he wore clung to the thick large muscles of his arms as they rested on the edge of the booth. Artificially black hair punched up the paleness of his face which had obviously been enhanced with makeup, as had his thick dark eyelashes.

Like her, he had an earring through his brow, although his was silver. His ears also sported a variety of piercings and when he smiled, the wink of silver in his tongue promised her more pleasure.

A vamp wannabe? she wondered. Or just out for a night of play?

Finishing her blood, Stacia rose from her stool and walked toward the booth, but didn't immediately engage the young man. While the direct approach generally worked best, sometimes the hunt and chase was much more stimulating.

With the slightest glance his way—although enough to let him know he had been noticed—she sauntered past him to the dance floor, making sure to stay in his line of sight.

Once there, she released herself to the music, shifting to the hard beats. They were almost violent in their volume, the strength of the sound driving against her body until it was as if the throb of the bass had melded with her heartbeat.

She moved her hips, gyrating in rhythm to the pulse. Raised her hands, which lifted the hem of her black leather vest to expose the pale expanse of her flat midriff and the woven ring of gold through her navel.

Warmth came against her skin as a hand snaked around her waist and dragged her to a rock-hard body.

Looking up over her shoulder, she smiled as she saw the young Goth man behind her. Felt the strength and size of his physique against her petite frame.

As she moved her backside, pressing into him, she realized she had made a good choice. He was just what she needed to welcome her to New York City.

Chapter 4

Okay, so Stacia had basically dissed him. That still didn't change the fact that she was absolutely stunning. A goddess.

Considering that she was an elder, maybe that wasn't so far from the truth. In the vampire world, the elders were like gods.

From the corner of his eye, Blake took in all of her. The black leather she wore looked as if it were painted on the womanly curves of her body. Her nearly black hair was a shock of dark against the ivory of her skin. Sleek and cropped close to her skull, it exposed the perfect shells of her ears with an assortment of golden earrings.

As she twirled around the rather large Goth, laughing and playing her sexual games, the golden ring at her brow winked enticingly as did the golden ring through her navel.

She was something to behold, he realized, although nothing like Meghan who was like the light of the sun to Stacia's dark night. Fun to Stacia's fear since despite his earlier denial, on some level he was afraid of her.

Stacia could take his life with a flick of her finger. He would be foolish not to respect her and yet...

There was something different about her tonight. Something almost...human. He tuned out the young woman next to him and kept an eye on Stacia.

Not that she needed protection.

The young man with her might be a mountain of muscle, but he was mortal. Blake knew that much from the lack of power that came from the Goth. He was no match for Stacia, even if she was such a little thing.

He liked his women petite, Blake realized, recalling Meghan. Stacia was of a like height, but much more womanly with all those delectable curves.

Not that he was interested, Blake thought. He had enough problems with women in his life and without a backward glance, abandoned his dance companion.

Unlike Stacia, who seemed to have few problems finding a man, he thought as he stalked back to the bar, wondering why Stacia's intense dance with the Goth was bothering him so.

Maybe because Stacia's idea of a dance was...

He gulped, fighting the thrum of power she was releasing as she played with the Goth. He wasn't the only one feeling it, he realized as a surge of awakening told him that the other vampires in the club were also experiencing it. Tapping into the spill of her elder power, like chum for vampires.

Only the price to be paid for fully experiencing a kiss of that power could be lethal if the elder was so inclined.

Tonight, Stacia seemed intent on satisfying other needs, Blake thought, sipping on his wine as he watched her sway against the young man. Run her hands up his arms and over his exaggerated muscles.

He glanced down at his own arms. Lean and mean, he had nothing to be ashamed of, he thought, and returned his attention to the antics of Stacia and the Goth.

The young man was clearly smitten, unaware that beneath the body that he was so eagerly moving his hands all over was destructive power. Strength beyond that of anyone else in the room. Lust and desire that would ensnare you in its grasp, but then drain you dry if you gave in to it.

Blake sucked in a shaky breath, feeling the pull of her even across the distance of the club. Feeling himself harden and rise from the spillover of her ardor.

But he was not alone. As Stacia faced the bar, their gazes connected and he realized that she sensed his awakening passion. Passion stronger than that of the puny mortal with her.

While facing him, she raised her hand up to caress the Goth's face.

Blake felt the sweep of her hand as if against his own cheek. So soft. Cold.

She shifted her hips back and forth, and he had to grip the edge of the bar as that movement transferred itself to him and his erection strained painfully against the tight fabric of his jeans.

All the time, Stacia kept her gaze locked with his, clearly aware of her effect on him. Increasing her caresses and movements until he was nearly undone and she finally broke free from the Goth, done with his weak mortality.

She began to head his way, well aware that the pleasure of Blake's body and blood would surpass that of any puny mortal.

And Lord help him, he was ready to give in to her despite knowing it would be a mistake. A major mistake.

Stacia could never love anyone.

But love was highly overrated anyway, wasn't it? Blake thought as he rose from the stool and walked toward her.

The Goth clearly didn't like being left behind wanting. He grabbed hold of Stacia's arm, spun her around so that he could voice his displeasure.

With the barest movement of her arm, Stacia broke free from the young man and raised her hand. The Goth dropped to his knees, his face reflecting disbelief at his seeming inability to control his own body.

Blake approached and despite his better judgment,

laid his hand over Stacia's. Barely half a foot taller than her, it took little for him to bend down and whisper in her ear, "Let the young fool go, luv."

Stacia shot him a look, but beneath his hand, the hum of power surging outward warmed his palm. The young man was swaying and beginning to turn blue, but Blake couldn't tell just what Stacia was doing to him until she broadcast the vision she had in her mind.

He saw it then, compliments of Stacia's power. She was encircling the Goth's heart, slowly crushing the life from it. If she didn't release her hold on him, the foolish boy would soon be dead.

"If you finish this—"

"*When* I finish this," she corrected and almost as if for the fun of it, gave the young man a shake.

"Let him go. You've proven your point," he urged and surprisingly, she did as he asked.

"Thank you," Blake said, but Stacia shook her head at his words.

"Don't thank me, Blake. If you don't know by now, I expect payment for that request," she said and was about to walk away when the Goth's friends surrounded them.

As two of them helped their friend back to the booth, another two blocked their way. Their stances were fight-ready, their looks surly.

Blake raised his hand. "You don't want to do this," he suggested in low tones.

"That's right. You don't want to do this. At least, not here," Foley, the owner of the bar, said as he approached the group.

The two young men looked at Foley and one of them nodded and said, "Let's take it outside."

Blake was about to protest that there was no need, only Stacia and the two men were already stalking away to a back exit to the alley.

Shit, he thought, following them. He hated being a hero.

Chapter 5

Anger pushed her to rashness. *So* not a good thing, Stacia thought as she thrust open the back door of the club. It rebounded against the wall with a loud clang before she stepped into the alley. She reminded herself that too many a vampire had let emotion lead them to a stupid act which cost them their lives.

But she couldn't let these two go unpunished. A little infliction of pain would suffice to satisfy her honor and temper.

Bright moonlight spilled onto the cracked cement walls and the asphalt on the floor in the alley. The better to see their blood with, she thought and turned to face the two young men as they took up positions on either side of her. Blake had followed them out as well, but merely leaned against the wall by the door and crossed his arms nonchalantly, a bored look on his face.

The stupid-looking muscle-bound one called out to him, "Are you just going to stand there while we kick your girl's ass?"

"Bullocks, mate. That woman is so going to make you suffer. I'm just here to make sure you're still breathing when she's done," Blake said and after wagged a finger in Stacia's direction.

"None of your nasties with these children. We wouldn't want mum and dad to have to spend too much money on therapy," he teased and actually dragged out a chuckle from her, but that humor was short-lived.

The thick-necked oaf and his friend clearly didn't think it funny because they suddenly decided to advance on Blake, until she grabbed the hand of one as he walked away from her. With a deft flick of her wrist, she had his arm bent back at a painful enough angle that the young man slowly sank to his knees.

His friend, seeing that he needed assistance, immediately swung a punch in her direction, but she caught his fist in her hand, stopping him midswing. Exerting pressure, she reveled in the wince he gave a second before she used her vamp strength and sent him flying back against the brick wall.

His body impacted with a dull thud and momentarily stunned, he sank down onto the floor of the alley beside where Blake stood.

Blake looked down at him in amusement. "Score two for the little chit."

"Bitch," his friend shouted and despite her painful grip on his arm, he, too, attempted a punch. A second later, he found himself lying on the floor beside his friend, groaning.

"Had enough, mates?" Blake said, bending down to talk to the two, but they refused to quit the fight.

Since Blake was the closest target, the first youth rose and wrapped Blake up in a bear hug, easily picking him up with his much greater size. He waddled with him in his grasp until they were close to Stacia, but by then Blake had broken free.

Blake placed his back against hers as the two men circled around them, not that she needed his protection. As the men came at them time and time again, Stacia and Blake struck out, inflicting damage.

It was a little odd to have Blake guarding her back. No one had done that in a long time. It was almost—reassuring, she thought as the two men swarmed around them, darting toward them and back out like nasty gnats. Annoying, but harmless.

"This is rather ho-hum," she said to Blake as she cut short a jab to her face and followed up with a sharp blow to the youth's nose. Stacia smiled at the satisfying sound of cartilage cracking, not that it stopped her attacker.

From behind her came the sound of the meaty impact of a fist and Blake staggered against her back.

"Just dandy, luv. I always love getting my face kicked in by some nancy boy," Blake muttered.

She chuckled again, but it distracted her enough that her assailant landed a punishing blow to her ribs. The anger she had been trying to corral broke free.

With a surge of vamp speed, she landed multiple blows to his face until the young man dropped his arms and just stood there. He seemed stunned for a moment, blood running down his face from the assorted cuts her blows had opened up and from his broken nose. His blood was bright red against his skin. Glistening in the moonlight. Flowing freely.

When he recovered from that temporary daze and came at her again, the blood was all Stacia smelled. Warm on her hands as she connected with his face time and time again. Each blow drawing yet more blood. Inflicting greater pain until with one last shot to the man's ribs, he staggered to his knees.

Stacia didn't waste a moment, grabbing him from behind and yanking his head to the side to expose his throat. Her fangs burst forth from her mouth, eager for the taste of him. She sank her fangs deep, enjoying the rich taste of his life. Over and over she pulled at his throat, the heat of his blood warming her. Filling her undead body with energy. She savored the moan he gave, tinged with both pain and desire from her vampire's kiss.

Between her own legs came an answering throb as his blood and desire awakened that part of her, as well.

She wanted more, she thought, sucking even harder while snaking her hand down and finding the young man's rock-hard erection. She wanted to ride him until she heard his last gasping breath of life.

But suddenly, Blake was there. Yanking her hand away and trapping it in his. Thrusting his arm between her and the young man, who dropped to the ground, alive, but unconscious. The ragged bite on his neck already beginning to heal.

She turned on Blake, shocked at his intervention. "You dare to challenge me?"

"Luv, I couldn't let you do it," he said, the tones of his voice low and conciliatory, but insufficient to assuage the frustration caused by his meddling.

Fisting her hand into the soft leather of his jacket, she picked him up off the ground with her greater strength and held him in the air. With a shake, she said, "Then you'll take his place, beloved."

Chapter 6

He had never seen her in such a fine anger, Blake thought, while dangling nearly a foot above the ground. Trying to placate her, he said, "Stacia, please—"

With a flick of her hand, he flew across the alleyway and into the wall. His head connected with a loud crack and stars swam before his eyes. He struggled for a hold on the wall, but soon found himself sliding down to sit on the cold stone floor of the alley.

His vision wavered and he forced himself to focus on something as he tried to regain his senses. Her boots. Black. Shiny. Pointy. Coming toward him in a wicked quick beat. Giving him no time, he thought as she once again grabbed the front of his jacket and picked him up as if he didn't weigh a thing. With him in her grasp, she entered the bar.

His head was still whirling and something wet ran down the back of it. She walked with him without laboring, her immense elder power giving her strength beyond his. As he shook his head to try and clear his senses, a lot of other things came to him about what the elders could do, creating a cold knot of fear in his stomach.

You can't even begin to guess. Stacia's thoughts entered his head as she obviously knew what he was thinking.

I didn't want any problems for you. Things are different now, he offered in apology, but Stacia's only response was to motion with him to the door before them.

Even in his dazed state he recognized the entrance to one of the back rooms in the Blood Bank. Foley kept them for his special visitors who would pay a fee for the use of the specially equipped rooms. Not that Foley would dare ask a fee from Stacia or, for that matter, stop her from doing what she would with him in that room.

"Stacia, please—"

"Don't beg, beloved. It's so unbecoming," she said as she raised her hand and thrust open the door without even touching it. She strode in, shut the door with another flick of her hand and tossed him onto the metal cot along one wall.

He wouldn't beg again, Blake thought, even as Stacia exerted her elder's power to keep him immobile as she shackled him to the thick iron frame of the bed.

Blake watched as she walked to the far wall which was equipped with an assortment of toys and other devices. As Stacia stood there, considering what to choose, her mental hold on him relaxed and he pulled against the leather cuffs which had him spread-eagled on the bed. But couldn't free himself.

The cuffs and bed had clearly been chosen with a vampire in mind since they were thick and sturdy. He realized he could not get loose and bit back his concern as Stacia turned and displayed a rather large and nasty-looking dagger.

She sauntered over, the blade held upright in her hands, plainly visible as if to inflict some mental torture. "Do you know what you did, Blake?"

He wouldn't show her he was worried. With what he hoped was a careless shrug—which was kind of difficult when one was lashed to the bedposts—he calmly said, "I was only trying to help."

Stacia laughed harshly. "Help? You helping me? That's rich."

"It's the truth. Things are changing around here," he said again, but Stacia would hear none of it.

She brought the blade down to his cheek. The metal was cold against his skin. Leaning close, she said, "Since when do we care whether we drain a human?"

"Since maybe some of us know that it's wrong?" he shot back, remembering all too painfully what had happened with Meghan.

Stacia was too omnipotent not to pick up on what he was feeling. Bringing the knife to his wrist, she slipped it beneath the leather and said, "Intriguing. You actually feel...regret and love? You fancied yourself in love?"

He felt the prick of the knife lightly against his skin and then the cool air of the night as she sliced open one sleeve of his jacket, then reached over and quickly did the same to the other sleeve.

He met her gaze as she paused, the knife poised above his midsection and directly above a most delicate area. As she slipped the blade beneath the hem of his T-shirt, he shivered from the cold and from the anxiety he couldn't contain. One little slice of the knife—

Not yet, beloved. I'll have my satisfaction first.

"Well, that's good, luv. I'd hate to pass without at least getting a look," he said, determined to not let her be totally in control.

"What? A look? You want a look before I geld you?" she asked with an uneasy chuckle and the knife wavered against his midsection.

"If that's the price to be paid for a slight misunderstanding, the least you can do is let me see if what's beneath all that sinful black leather is as beautiful as the rest of you," he said, and surprisingly, he meant it.

Stacia was a remarkably stunning woman with her exotic almond-shaped eyes, dark and filled with so much emotion. Right now, a slight furrow marred the space above the dark slashes of her brows and that one golden earring. But then a glitter crept into her eyes and was followed by a wide smile across her full lips.

"You are ballsy."

He chuckled, shot a look down at his naked parts and said, "Definitely."

She laughed out loud at that, strode away from him and back to the wall with all the assorted gadgets and accessories. She placed the dagger back into its holder, paused for a second before turning to look at him. She tapped her lips with one finger and said, "You've been naughty, Blake. Very, very naughty."

Blake sensed the change in her. The playfulness in her tone that said he had reached past her anger to something else. Something way more interesting, he thought, wondering about the complex creature that she was.

As she turned away from him and back toward the wall, he realized she was working at something with her hands. A second later, she shrugged off the vest she had been wearing, exposing the long, slender line of her back. The perfect expanse of creamy skin that he suddenly itched to touch, wondering whether it would feel like smooth alabaster beneath his fingers.

He had been so drawn to that sight, that he didn't realize she had grabbed a cat-o-nine tails from the wall until she stood before him, the weapon held in her hand.

But even then, his mind was not so much on the pain she might inflict with it as the truly rewarding sight of her naked. Her breasts were full. Her nipples hard with her passion and the color of golden honey, a surprise given her dark coloring. He wondered how they might taste and didn't even realize he had asked the question until she said, "You wanted to see and now you want to taste?"

He salivated at the thought of it, but couldn't voice anything else as she brought the cat-o-nine tails to rest on his thigh, which immediately grabbed his attention.

"You are...engaging," she said as she slowly trailed the leather strips studded with small metal balls up his thigh until they rested against his erection. The contrast of the smooth leather snaking around him together with the cold of the hard metal balls was a shock.

"I could be much more engaging if you let me go," he said, because all he could think about was having her even if there would be pain afterward. Hell, with women there was always pain afterward.

Do you fear nothing? she asked silently as she continued to fondle him with the cat-o-nine tails, yanking a moan from him with the caresses.

Blake met her gaze and in there, he thought he caught a reflection of something familiar. Something they might share. "I fear living the rest of my life without love."

She stopped her caresses and a spark of anger came to life in her gaze. "What do you know about living without love? You've been undead but a second compared to my life."

"That's right. But at least I've had a taste of it. Can you say the same?"

Chapter 7

Stacia wanted to lash out at Blake. Shred his flesh and cut his manhood to bits for reminding her of all that she did not have. Only...

There was something about him she had never noticed before, besides his marvelous body. As she had walked toward him before, she had realized that not even Michelangelo could have done a better job of sculpting the chiseled lines of his body and face. He might be of average height and nothing like the men she normally preferred, but his body was definitely not average.

From those lean, defined muscles to his truly extraordinary erection, Blake was an exceptional specimen. Physically, that was.

And now it occurred to her that he was remarkable in other ways. That he had the kind of spirit she had found lacking in men for nearly two thousand years. Because of that, she wasn't about to pass up this opportunity.

Tossing aside the cat-o-nine tails, she replaced it with her hand and said, "Do you think you can show me love, Blake? Do you think you have what it takes?"

His amazing blue eyes, nearly the color of sapphire now from his passion, trained on the actions of her hand as she stroked him. "Do you think that's what it takes, Stacia?"

She stopped and yanked her hand away, as if punished, but then picked up her chin defiantly. "What do you want, Blake?"

"Let me loose, luv, and I'll show you."

Stacia wavered, torn between setting him free and her original plan to geld him. The latter would be much safer for her emotions, she realized, but not nearly as satisfying as the former.

But both options unsettled her, making her wonder if the other elders were right in saying that she should let go of that last vestige of humanity that created such disquiet within her.

She took a step back from him, torn between violence and desire. Between allowing herself respite in his arms or the satisfaction of vengeance.

"Don't run, Stacia," he said and yanked at the shackles holding his arms, as if sensing her sudden indecision.

But even as he repeated his entreaty, she was grabbing her vest and running out the door, chased by the sound of his voice as he called out, "You can't run forever, luv."

Stacia stalked back and forth across the parquet floor in Diego's living room, her heels striking a sharp staccato beat with each step.

"*Amor,* I'm going to have to refinish that floor if you keep that up," Diego said with amusement.

She whirled to face him. He sat at an angle in a large wing chair, one leg tossed over the arm of the chair, the other stretched out before him. A glass filled with a rioja from his native Spain dangled from one hand. He was the picture of an indolent royal, which, of course, he had been in another life.

Maybe that was why out of all the other wannabe humans at the Blood Bank, the two of them understood each other the best. In past lives they had both been part of the cream of society. It was how they had met nearly three hundred years earlier. And of course, they had both become vampires due to a loved one's betrayal.

"He's absolutely insane, Diego. Do you know that?" She snapped up the hand that held her glass of wine and took a long sip.

"You know those English fops. Forever lamenting lost love like in those awful poems—"

"Bloody awful," she confirmed and took up her

pacing again, but at a much slower tempo, taking an occasional sip of wine every now and then.

"Matches his bloody awful hair and that wardrobe with all the black..." Diego paused as he took in her attire—yet another ensemble of black leather, only this time decorated with finely wrought silver filigree.

"Sorry, *mi amiga.* I forgot your penchant for cowhide," Diego quipped and finished off his glass of wine.

"As disagreeable as it may be, he has that certain bad-boy charm that humans are so susceptible to," she said with a disdainful sniff.

"But not you, *amiga?* So you don't care where he's been hiding himself the last few days?" Diego asked with an arch of a sandy-colored brow and a knowing gleam in his gray eyes.

"He's smart to make himself scarce because the two of us have something to finish. When I do find him—"

"You'll make him suffer?"

His question hung unanswered and as she examined his face, she realized her lordly friend might actually like to see Blake tormented. "You have issues with him?"

The shrug Diego gave was an attempt at carefree, but the movement was a trifle stiff, plus she could sense the angry vibes mingling with his vampire power. "Thanks to his betrayal, Esperanza was kidnapped and killed."

"And yet you let him live?" she questioned and walked to the sofa beside Diego, sat down and trained her gaze on his face, unable to believe that her friend would not have sought vengeance for his lover's death.

"In the end, he nearly died to save my life and that of my charge, so I tolerate his presence."

"Your charge? As in Meghan? The child I've seen around here?" she asked, pondering why Blake would play the hero since in all the decades she had known him, Blake had only thought of himself.

Diego shook his head and tsked. "She's a child to you with all your years, but to everyone else..."

"And why would Blake..." She stopped as a look came to Diego's face that explained everything. "He fancied himself in love with her."

She tried to tamp down the jealousy she felt with that realization. After all, what she and Blake had shared...

But they hadn't shared it. She had run away, unwilling to risk exploring the feelings Blake roused in her.

"Do you think he can love? After so many years—"

"Anyone can love, Stacia. They just have to be willing to open their heart to it."

Heart? she thought. Most would say she hadn't possessed a heart in a long time and yet...

"So where has Blake been hiding? At that new club?"

"The Lair?" Diego asked, and shook his head. "He's probably holed up in his tiny room, waiting for you to calm down."

"I'm calm now," she told her friend, only he just chuckled.

"*Sí*. I can tell how cool and composed you are. So are you going there?"

"Going where?" she asked, leaning forward to snag the bottle of rioja from the coffee table and pour herself another glass.

"To Blake's room. It's right next to Gramercy Park. Probably makes him feel like he's in proper old England," he scoffed and held out his glass so she would pour him some more wine, as well.

She eyed him, wondering what her friend was about. "Why are you telling me this?"

Diego smiled, but there was nothing friendly about it. "Because in the nearly three hundred years that we've been friends, you've never left any business unfinished. Especially a challenge to your power."

Chuckling, she brought the glass to her lips and took a sip. The rioja was spirited and refreshing, reminding her of Blake surprisingly. Not that Diego wanted to hear that. She suspected he was only too eager for her to finish her business with Blake because he thought it would include inflicting some punishment on the punk vampire.

But as she sipped her wine, it occurred to her that she had much better things to do with him. That maybe, just maybe, he might be the one to make a difference in her life for the first time in a long time.

Downing the rest of her wine in one big gulp, she rose from the sofa. "So are you going to give me directions? I'd so hate to disappoint you by not settling my score with Blake."

Chapter 8

Blake had thought it best to avoid the Blood Bank and Stacia for a few days. Hopefully the time would give her the opportunity to cool down and give him a chance to figure out just what he was feeling for her.

It was insane really to be feeling anything but fear. She was an elder. She could end his life by exerting only the smallest amount of her power. Only she hadn't. Even with her extreme anger the other night, she had spared him.

She hadn't even truly harmed him, except of course for the humiliation of being found naked and bound by one of Foley's people and of course, the desire for her that had gone painfully unsatisfied.

A desire that called to him every time he thought of her. Remembered how magnificent she had looked with her breasts unbound after she had removed her vest. The lean lines of her body and as he had noticed when she danced with the Goth, the ring of gold threaded through her belly button.

He grew hard just imagining kissing her there.

Tonguing that golden ring and then moving lower until...

A sharp rap came at his door, disrupting his fantasy. He wondered who it could be since he didn't get many visitors up on his rooftop.

He stalked to the door, eager to be rid of them and back to his musings about Stacia. Throwing the door open, he was alternately surprised and fearful to see her there. "Well, luv, fancy that. I was just thinking about you and here you are."

"Really? And you're not in the least bit worried about why I'm here?" she asked, one brow arched in a way that made the ring of gold there almost wink at him impudently.

He stepped aside and held his hand out in invitation. "I'm assuming you're here to finish up our business of the other night."

Stacia chuckled as she sauntered in, the sway of her hips in all that black leather mesmerizing. Once she was inside, she placed her hands on her hips and looked around, taking note of the collection of cast-offs in his small rooftop home.

On the floor, thick oriental rugs that had seen better days, but were ruthlessly clean and of high quality. Rich mahogany furniture filled the small space, from the oddly matching tables scattered here and there which held an assortment of candles to the jewel in his room—a large four-poster bed piled high with a sumptuous collection of linens.

"Very nice," she said and headed to the French doors he had picked up from a nearby demolition site and installed to give him access to the rest of the roof. She opened the French doors and stepped outside.

He followed, walking with her to the edge of the building which was directly across from Gramercy Park. In the early spring night, a sliver of moon illuminated the park where the branches of the trees were still bare of any growth. She looked at him and then around to the wrought-iron chairs and table on the roof, as well as the assorted pots for plants.

"I didn't take you for a nature boy," she said and laid a hand on his chest, stroking him through the thin cotton of the T-shirt.

Blake shrugged as he said, "My family had a farm before..." He stopped, sensing it wasn't the time for recollections about his lineage, but when she looked up at him with her fathomless eyes, he sensed she wanted a connection. He picked up her hand and cradled her cheek, cold as the night and smooth. Like satin.

"You're very beautiful," he said and traced the edges of her full lips with his thumb.

"Do you think you're the first man who's ever told me that?" she said, a hint of scorn in her tone even as she raised the hand on his chest up to cup his jaw.

"No, but I'd like to be the last," he said with a broad grin.

He was irresistible, Stacia thought. Handsome and full of spirit. Passionate. Desire rose up, urging her to take the risk. To seek out the solace he might bring to her heart, and so she inched up on tiptoe and kissed him.

His lips were cold. Firm. He met her kiss tentatively at first, but then relaxed and soon his mouth opened on hers, tasting her. Begging her to open and allow him more, which she did, leaning into him as his tongue darted out to lick the edges of her lips and slip into her mouth. Dancing with her tongue until they were both straining against each other, needing more.

Arms wrapped around one another, they staggered back into his room and toward the bed, but at its edge he stopped and stepped back a bit. Looking down at her from his slightly greater height, he said, "I've waited too long to rush this."

"Me, too," she confessed.

With a nod, he slowly undressed her, his fingers skimming her skin as he slipped each button of her silk shirt free. She was naked beneath and as she shrugged off the shirt to expose herself to him, he gasped at the sight of her beauty.

Blake cupped her breasts in his hands. Strummed his thumbs across her nipples until she mewled a protest and then he replaced his hands with his mouth. Sucking at her, gently at first, but then just a bit harder as she cupped the back of his head to her.

Then he slowly sank to his knees, kissing a line down the center of her. His hands holding her hips as he dipped his tongue into her navel and after playfully tugged at the golden ring there with his teeth.

That tug sent a direct signal to the center of her. She moaned and sat back on the edge of the bed, her knees almost weak from the desire he had awoken.

"Easy, luv," he said as he worked open her black leather pants and then slipped his hands beneath to drag them off.

Blake paused to admire all that he had revealed. To marvel at the pale skin between her legs. At his perusal, she parted her thighs, exposing the deeper coral of her lips, glistening with her need. With a half glance at her, he slipped between her legs, kissed her there.

She let out a ragged sigh, but cupped his head to her as he pleasured her with his mouth and tongue, until he felt the quickening beneath his fingers, and his own erection twitched to remind him that it, too, needed more.

Vamp speed was a good thing, he thought, as he tossed off his shirt and jeans and returned to give her one last lick before he rose and positioned himself at her opening.

Stacia watched the emotions splash across his face as he gazed down at her, hesitating as if asking permission. With the slight shift of her hips, she invited him in.

He moved slowly, restraining himself so as to satisfy her. Conscious of her every need as he slipped his hands up her body to caress her breasts. Bent and took her mouth with a kiss that mimicked the motion of his hips, until she was gasping for breath and her heart thundered in her chest.

She picked up her knees and cradled his hips, increasing the penetration of his thrusts and he quickened his tempo then. Strengthened the force of his thrusts until she had to hold on to his shoulders to keep with him. Nearly panting with the intensity of his lovemaking.

As his gaze locked with hers, she realized he was striving for something besides physical satisfaction. Something was lacking within him much as it was within her. And so she raised her lips to his, wanting to give him that. Wanting to take it from him, as well. "Love me, Blake."

With one arm braced on the bed to keep his weight off her, he cupped her head with his free hand and whispered, "You have it, Stacia. You have it, luv."

The kiss that followed sent them both over the edge, but even as they lay there afterward, damp and sated, she needed more and he gave it. Time and time again they made love until the first fingers of a rosy dawn crept into the night sky and the sounds of birds tittering out in the park reminded them that it was time to rest.

Blake snuggled her against his side and she went there willingly, satisfaction of both a physical and mental kind granting her peace for the moment.

As she lay there, savoring the lean lines of his body and the comfort of his arms, Stacia wanted to ask if this was forever, but after two thousand years of existence, she knew forever was promised to no one. So instead she said, "Is this love, Blake?"

A boyish grin slowly blossomed on his face and traveled up to his deep blue eyes, which sparkled with promise. "I certainly hope so, luv."

The smile shook something loose inside of her and for the first time in centuries, Stacia imagined love was possible for her. Inching upward, she whispered against his lips, "So do I," and kissed him.

* * * * *

Turn the page to start reading an excerpt from DEATH CALLS, *the next book in Caridad Piñeiro's* THE CALLING *miniseries.*

DEATH CALLS
CARIDAD PIÑEIRO

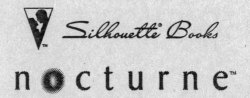

Silhouette Books

nocturne™

Chapter 1

Like the phantom pain of a lost limb, the memory of Ryder's bite lingered, reminding her of what he'd done. Reminding her that she'd begged for his violence.

There was no scar at her neck. No fresh wound, raw and bleeding. Instead, the pain was deep inside, as alive in her heart as the day two years ago when her lover had first revealed his vampire nature.

Before Ryder, she hadn't allowed herself to feel anything for anyone, not since her father's death. That she had lowered her defenses and made love with him only to find out he was a vampire had awoken the rage and anger she had thought under control. Dealing with it had been difficult.

Now, it was almost as painful to acknowledge where their two-year love affair had led them—to the wreckage of her carefully reconstructed life.

Diana grabbed her shot of Cuervo and downed it in one gulp. Then she immediately signaled the bartender for another. But she only stared at the drink in front of her, fingers splayed on the scarred black surface of the bar.

The Blood Bank was a favorite haunt of those in Manhattan's vampire subculture and a great place if one wanted to offer themself up as a treat. But after the day she'd had she only wanted to lick her wounds and hopefully not add any fresh ones.

She didn't want anyone to put the bite on her. Not even Ryder. Not again. Okay, *maybe* not again, she confessed when the heated recollection of their passion replaced the warmth of the tequila.

A reaction that reminded her all too vividly of why she was here, bleeding on the inside and just barely in control on the surface. A combination sure to bring trouble.

By anyone else's standards, it had been an ordinary day. Diana had met her best friend outside a favorite Italian restaurant, a place Diana hadn't been to in months. When, she'd wondered, had she stopped going to her normal haunts and started going almost exclusively to Ryder's?

She'd dismissed the thought upon seeing Sylvia. There had been something different about her friend. She'd seemed positively radiant. Sylvia's coffee-brown eyes had glittered with joy and her smooth olive skin bore a vibrant blush. Eventually, Diana noticed the swell of her belly. Her friend not only confirmed the happy news, but asked Diana to be godmother to the baby.

Diana had been happy for Sylvia. At least, that's what she'd told herself initially.

Until Sylvia glanced down at her belly and rubbed her hand lovingly over it. That motherly gesture drove an arrow of pain deep into the middle of Diana's heart.

Her doubts about Ryder, about their relationship, overwhelmed her. Doubts, that if she was honest, she'd been having for months, since her brother had announced the coming birth of his own child. Diana would never know the sensation of a baby growing and moving within her, of seeing herself fecund with child. At least, not if she stayed with Ryder. He was a vampire, undead. He couldn't bestow life.

"Are you going to put that drink out of its misery or let it sit there all night?"

Brought back to the present, Diana glared at Foley, the owner of the Blood Bank, as he perched on the bar stool next to her. As always, he was lethally elegant in a fitted black suit that punched up the paleness of his skin and hair and elongated the already sparse lines of his body. With a shrug meant to dissuade his attention, she replied, "I didn't know an inanimate object could feel misery."

The vampire's clear gray eyes darkened. With one

finger, he traced her heart-and-dagger tattoo through the fabric of her suit. "They do when they could be in something as delicious as you."

Diana snared his hand and bent his thumb back at an awkward angle. "Don't go there."

Foley's grin didn't waver, although she knew that even with his vampire strength, she was likely causing some hurt. "Did you get that tattoo to prove how tough you are, Special Agent Reyes?"

She laughed harshly and increased the tension of her hold. "I got it to remind me of the pain."

"You enjoy it, don't you?" he asked. A sly look slid into his gaze, hinting that he rather liked the hurt she was currently inflicting on him. She let him go.

"I enjoy dishing it out."

In truth, the tattoo was a reminder not to act impulsively, a trait she had been accused of more than once. After a night of too much tequila, she'd gotten the tattoo to remind herself to guard against the pain she had suffered after losing her boyfriend. Only later did she realize that the knot of sorrow within her had been about the death of her father and all that she believed in. Justice. Honor. Happiness. Herself.

Sitting here, drowning her misery in tequila now, as much as she'd done at nineteen, warned her she was in danger of losing herself again as she had nearly a decade earlier when her dad had died.

"Bad day at the office, Special Agent Reyes?" Foley waved for a drink—a shot glass filled with liquid the color of ripe, succulent cherries. Freshly drawn blood.

"A nouveau Italian straight from Mulberry Street." He held the glass up in a toast.

Despite her earlier recollection about where one too many tequilas might lead her, she hoped a few more would create the right degree of numb. Help her forget about babies, husbands and houses filled with family— the kinds of things Ryder could never give her. She clicked her glass with Foley's and bolted back the Cuervo. The sting made her wince as the liquor burned its way down her throat. Slamming the glass onto the bar, she motioned for another.

"Extremely bad, I guess," Foley said, which only earned him a sidelong glance. He was sipping his drink slowly, savoring the grisly libation.

"What do you want?"

Foley leaned closer. So close that his chilled breath bathed the side of her face. With it came the metallic smell of blood. She almost gagged.

"Just to chat with a friend."

She gave him a forceful nudge in the ribs to remind him he had invaded her space. "You and I aren't—"

"Pals? Chums? Aren't you and Ryder…friendly?"

Ignoring him, she laid her hands on the bar's rough surface. Beneath her palms she registered the bumps, dents and gouges worn into it by misuse, by the violence for which the Blood Bank was known in the undead world. Again the phantom pain came to her neck and she inched her hand upward.

Foley ran the icy pad of his finger over the spot of the long-healed and invisible injury in a caress that made her skin crawl. "He's bitten you, hasn't he? More than once. And not just to feed. Yum." He smacked his lips with pleasure.

She yanked away from his touch, angry with his intrusion into her private life. "So what? Taking a survey?"

"With each bite his control over you grows. Your need for him intensifies until…"

You beg him to take you. To make you like him.

Which scared the shit out of her.

She prided herself on having learned control a long time ago. In the year following her father's death, she had lost her restraint and her identity in the ambience of places like the Blood Bank. It was only after waking one morning facedown in vomit, her younger brother passed out beside her, that she realized she was on the road to oblivion and taking her brother with her. She had mustered the strength to deal with her pain, to restore her sense of self and honor. It had taken her a long time to control her rebellion, to choose what she knew was right.

Lately she seemed to have less control over her emotions, over her choices, and worse, she didn't have a clue as to whether her relationship with Ryder was right or wrong. Which only partially explained why she found herself here, in a bar catering to the undead. Sharing a drink with a vampire who would drain her, given the right circumstances. Avoiding the lover who made her plead for a passion so intense....

That was the one thing she knew in her uncertain life. If Ryder was a drug, she was a Ryder junkie.

When she had first met him, Ryder had been living his life as humanly as possible. The attraction between them had been that of woman to man, man to woman. She hadn't known then just how hard it was for Ryder to control the beast within him. Or, worse, how much she would come to like the demon and what it made her feel.

The spot at her neck tingled again. When Ryder had been mostly human, she could tell herself their affair was right, but now that he was finally exploring his vampire powers, now that he was becoming less human she could no longer avoid the truth.

The change hadn't happened overnight. It was only in the past year or so, when they'd become more involved with Manhattan's other vampires, that Ryder had begun to change. She hadn't noticed at first, but recently it had become impossible to ignore. Ryder was darker and more powerful than she could have imagined. Worse yet, she liked his transformation. Too much.

And that was what troubled her the most—how much she wanted to share in his darkness, how much she craved the intense emotions only he could rouse. Was she losing herself to him?

Shaking her head to clear her thoughts, she half slipped off the high stool and tossed some money on the bar. Foley grabbed her arm, but she tugged free of his grasp. "Don't."

"Afraid?" His feral smile held a hint of fang.

But Foley's toothy smile didn't scare her. It only served to remind her of the vampire underworld that called to the darkness within her. A darkness she had thought she'd left behind after her father's death. One she didn't want to revisit.

"Screw you, Foley."

She walked away, chased by his laughter. Or maybe it was Foley calling, "Change your mind?" that pushed her onward.

She needed to be away from the Blood Bank and any other reminders of the surreal state of her life. She took a long walk before flagging a cab to go home.

Home. She needed to go home. Grab a pint of ice cream on the way and settle down to try to find some inner peace. Today had been just too normal. Lunch with a friend. The happiness and joy of Sylvia's coming child. The yearning for the contentment home and family could provide.

Even before Ryder, Diana hadn't thought much about that kind of life. Definitely not since becoming an FBI agent. Her career had taken up so much of her energy that she hadn't considered that at some point she might want…more.

But now she couldn't refute the possibilities and impossibilities. She had at one time thought she'd have a normal life. A husband and kids. Growing old. Dying. Everyday stuff.

She didn't want a life of the abnormal—one hidden beneath the surface of the city. She had existed like that once before and it had nearly consumed her.

Just as Ryder and his darkness would consume her if she didn't find a way to let go.

Monday was their night. His club was closed then, which meant they usually had the leisure of a long dinner, possibly a movie. Mortal things. Things that people who were dating regularly did.

Like making love. A maybe-not-so-mortal thing with them.

Was that why she had called tonight to tell him she didn't want to see him?

She'd been that blunt. Diana wasn't the kind of woman who made excuses.

And he wasn't the kind of man to…

But he wasn't a man anymore, Ryder reminded himself as he perused the streets from the balcony of his apartment. Across the East River, the large red Pepsi and Silvercup Studio signs glowed. The erratic string of lights from the bridge and Roosevelt Island tramway twinkled. In the water there were a few scattered boats, not many.

It was late, although in the city that never slept, the activity was incessant.

Where was Diana in all that activity? Holed up in her

office working on a case? Asleep in her apartment? Or somewhere else?

The last possibility bothered him more than he liked to admit. He had never considered himself a jealous man. But then again, he had never met a woman as complex and independent and as deliciously dark as Diana.

Ryder grew hard and his fangs elongated as he re-called their last bout of sex. She'd moved beneath him, pleading for his possession. For his bite.

Her blood had been sweet, spicing his mouth as she'd cried out her completion. He had become nearly feral with feeding from her body as he'd driven into her. Her blood, providing him…so much life.

He growled and shook his head to chase away the demon, the animal that had almost not let up the other night. He had come close to draining her. Had nearly made her like him, because she called to him like nothing else in his undead life. Now, he couldn't just stand there, wondering.

He sprung over the ledge of his balcony like a gymnast vaulting over a horse and landed on the balcony of the floor below, where Melissa—the doctor whose family legacy was to care for his vampire health and serve as his keeper—now lived with her husband.

He caught but a glimpse of her, belly large with child. She stroked a hand across her extended abdomen with a beatific smile on her face. A moment later, her husband—Diana's younger brother—Sebastian walked into the room, a similar grin on his features as he laid his hand over hers.

Ryder couldn't linger. The scene was too painful a reminder of the life taken from him so long ago. Of the life he would be stealing from Diana if they continued their relationship.

Or if he sired her.

After biting her the other night, he had been forced to acknowledge just how badly he wanted her with him forever. After more than a century of avoiding humans and their emotions, he had allowed himself to care for her. She had restored him. Made him alive again. Losing her...

He knew pain. For close to one hundred and forty-three years, he had lived with the anguish of loved ones dying, of having everything familiar change. His response had been to shut himself off from other vampires, from humanity. From love.

But now, because of Diana, he was no longer alone. Would he be able to handle the pain of her death? Unsettled by those thoughts, he leaped down, floor by floor, to the street below. Once there, he hesitated, uncertain of where he would go. Unsure that it was wise to give in to the beast who longed for more than just seeing her.

For so long he had controlled his vampire nature and striven for a human life, the kind of life he had lost during the Civil War.

He didn't really understand how the sheltered existence he had so carefully built had become filled not only with Diana, but with an assortment of people and vampires who demanded he acknowledge what he was.

After despising his vampire nature for more than a century, he hadn't expected ever to enjoy the power and passion and strength that releasing the demon would bring. For so long, he had kept the beast at bay, afraid of what it could do. He had seen the aftermath of vampire violence against others, against himself.

A physician before a supposed act of kindness had turned him, he had devoted his life to healing, to saving others. He hated that the demon within was the total antithesis of what he had been—a good man.

But over the past two years, he had discovered that he could use his vampire powers for good—if he could control the violence that accompanied the demon. The violence it was becoming harder and harder to restrain around Diana. Was it because the beast didn't want to lose a mate after so much time alone?

Tonight the demon screamed for him to let it loose. Reluctantly he did. With a quick look to make sure no one was watching, he transformed. Long fangs erupted from his mouth and blood surged through his veins. All around him, colors and noises became more vibrant. Sounds sharper, almost painful to his heightened hearing. Smells, all those luscious smells, ripe around him. And beneath it all, the awareness of the humans close at hand, throbbing with life.

Speed beyond that of a mortal drove him. Where, he

didn't quite know. He just reveled in the freedom of the night. The piercing glow of the moon and stars lit his way. The chill of the night air flew against his heated skin. As he brushed past one human on a side street, the scent filled his nostrils. The thunder of heartbeat and blood called to him. Sweet blood, pulsing.

Ryder badly wanted a taste. He imagined sinking his fangs through fragile skin before his mortal side rose up, reining in the vampire and urging him to a nearby rooftop. Hurtling from one edifice to the next, he reached an old and narrow cobblestone alley in Tribeca. The Blood Bank.

Hunger gnawed at his stomach.

Ryder stared at the entrance to the club. He didn't normally frequent the place, not much caring for Foley, the owner, or for the other vampires who so blithely indulged their baser instincts there, without a care. Without conscience. Totally unlike the vampires he had befriended in the past year. They tried to live nearly human lives. They also refused to feed from humans and didn't sire others like themselves. At least, they usually didn't.

Ryder had learned from his new friends that despite their best intentions, sometimes the beast won out. Their experience had confirmed what he'd already known—balancing his mortal and demon sides required dedicated effort.

So now here he was, the pit of his stomach clenching at the thought of fresh blood. Saliva pooled in his mouth like that of a hungry man sitting at a feast. Shaking his

head, he took a deep breath to quell the demon's urges—
and smelled her.

Diana.

She had either been nearby recently or was still
close. Inhaling sharply, he picked up her scent and
threw himself over the ledge of the building. He landed
on his feet as quietly and gracefully as a panther on the
prowl.

Her smell grew stronger at ground level. Ryder
followed it to the door of the club, flashed some fang
to get past the bouncer and hurried within, eager for
even a glimpse.

She had made her feelings known. But one night
away from her…was like an eternity.

In the stifling lifeless air of the club, Diana's smell
strengthened and he followed it to the bar. She sat with
Foley, letting the vampire lean toward her, touch her.

Ryder fisted his hands, barely controlling the desire
to rip Foley's finger off.

With perverse satisfaction, he smiled as Diana did
some damage of her own, but Foley, sick animal that
he was, kind of liked it. *So do you,* his inner voice re-
buked. *You like the violence she hides at her core.*

Anger barely subdued, he stepped into the shadows.
The noise and music were too loud and uneven for him
to make out their discussion. Interminably long minutes
passed before Diana left.

Ryder hesitated, debating whether to follow Diana or
to beat Foley into monster mash. First, because the

vampire had touched Diana. Second, because Ryder had never liked Foley. He was everything Ryder hated and never wanted to be: a hedonistic animal, devoid of any mortal sensibilities.

And for some reason, Diana had ditched him for the undead cad.

Ryder's human side urged him to curb his resentment. After all, she had left the bar alone and rebuffed Foley's sole advance. But the demon... The demon damn well wanted some satisfaction.

Satisfaction that words wouldn't provide.

* * * * *

MAUREEN CHILD

ETERNALLY

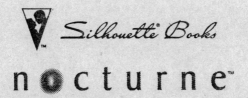

Silhouette Books

nocturne

Chapter 1

The body was found sprawled across Nicole Kidman's star on Hollywood Boulevard.

The tourists who'd spent all night partying, stumbled across what was left of Mary Alice Malone and ended their vacation with a whimper.

Sunlight glittered off camera lenses and shone down on the scene with a merciless glare. Pooled beneath the young woman's body, blood, in tiny dark rivers running from opened veins, crept into the gutter. The dead woman's wide blue eyes were frozen open in surprise, staring into the morning sky. Her left breast was gone, excised, as if by a talented yet depraved surgeon and her yellow silk blouse had been deliberately torn and arranged to expose the injury.

Belatedly a blanket was dropped over the body. But Mary Alice Malone was long past appreciating the privacy.

Ghoulish crowds jostled for position, cameras clicked and the unfortunate tourists wept. Police strung yellow crime scene tape and hid the pity in their eyes.

In L.A., one murder more or less—even one this vicious—hardly merited more than a mention on the local news channels and a small article on page two of the newspapers.

One man took note, though.

One man stood at the edge of the crime scene, letting his gaze sweep over the gathered mob. He knew his quarry was near. He'd recognized the killer's handiwork. He'd chased him before. And won. Now he would be forced to do it again.

And he knew that this murder was only the beginning.

The party was in full swing and Julie Carpenter swiveled on her desk chair to impotently glare at the door separating her suite from the rest of the house. Eardrum-shattering rock music pumped through the place, the bass making the walls tremble like a tired old man looking for a place to lie down.

Her head throbbing and her stomach growling, Julie surrendered to the inevitable. No way was she going to get any work done tonight.

"Thank you, Evan Fairbrook," she muttered and

tossed her pen down onto the legal-size pad of paper in front of her. Letting her head fall back, she stared at the ceiling through gritty eyes and called down one more curse onto the head of her ex-husband.

He couldn't be just a liar and a cheat. Oh, no. Wasn't enough just to sleep with her best friend and God knows how many other women in Cleveland. Evan, it turns out, was a *first-class* weasel. Before Julie had caught on, he'd emptied their bank accounts and stolen her car. If she'd had a dog, he would have kicked it.

She couldn't stay in Cleveland. Not with everyone looking at her, whispering about her, wondering how such a bright woman could have been so knuckle-dragging *stupid*. Julie sucked in a gulp of air and reminded herself that moving to California had been a good thing even though she missed her folks and her younger brother. She was in a new city, with a new job, surrounded by people fortunate enough to have never even *heard* of Evan Fairbrook.

No more suburban split level for her, either. Now she shared a historic old house high in the Hollywood Hills with two women who had become good friends. And, she was reinventing her career. The career that had supported Evan while he got his software business up and running.

The same software business that had folded the minute Evan milked all the money out of it and took that plane to Barbados. Julie's only hope now was that he got melanoma from romping around buck naked in the sun with her ex-best friend Carol.

"On his nose," she mused, smiling. "He should get a big, black hairy mole on his nose. Or maybe another body part he's equally fond of. Yeah. And then it should rot and fall off. The body part, not the mole. Slowly."

As curses went, it was one of her better ones, she thought, enjoying the mental image of Evan standing helplessly watching as his prized member swayed, tilted and dropped to the sand. As for Carol, the treacherous witch, it was enough of a curse that she was with Evan in the first place.

Julie blew out a breath and snorted. "Good for me." A year after Evan had screwed her over, she was able to see the humor in the situation. Sort of. Her pride had been dinged a little—okay, crushed, stomped and spit on—but once Evan was gone from her life, she'd been forced to admit that she hadn't really missed him. So what did that say about her?

She shook her head. Man, it was way too late to do any soul searching. Instead she'd eat the last of the Coney Island Waffle Cone ice cream in the freezer. She got up and headed for the door leading from her suite to the hallway connecting it to the kitchen of the huge old house. The mother-in-law suite she occupied in the 1920's Craftsman-style house was way at the back of the building, usually giving her the privacy she preferred.

She'd been lucky to find this place. Number one, she

hated apartment living. But more than that, being a freelance writer for the *L.A. Times* meant she needed a home base that was flexible. She did a lot of traveling and having housemates meant she didn't have to worry about her place while she was gone. Plus, she had company when she wanted it and privacy when she didn't.

Eventually, though, she'd like to move to the beach. And she'd take summers off. And do some damn sand frolicking herself.

Her cell phone rang before she could open her door and she checked caller ID before answering. "Hi, Kate."

"Hi." Kate Davies, one of Julie's housemates whispered into the phone, her voice almost lost in the slam of music still pounding through the house. "Hey, what do you want to eat tonight?"

Julie smiled. Living with two women who considered splitting an M&M a walk on the wild side had its fringe benefits. Neither Kate nor their other housemate, Alicia Walker *ever* ate if they could help it. And since they were determined to maintain their chic, skeletal look, whenever they went out on dates—which, let's face it, was a lot more often than Julie did—they brought a doggy bag back for her.

"Where'd he take you tonight?" Julie asked, hoping for a decent steak for once. If Kate or Alicia brought her back one more box of sushi, she'd sprout gills.

"Oh," Kate whispered, "you'd love it. Ruth's Chris. Just breathing in here I think I've gained two pounds."

"Thank God. Meat."

"So, what'll it be? Filet mignon?"

Julie sighed. "I think I just had an orgasm."

Laughter spilled through the phone. "Baked potato or garlic mashed?"

"Please. Garlic mashed. Definitely." Not like she had to watch her breath or anything. "Order the steak rare to allow for heating up later. And if he's willing to spring for dessert, anything chocolate."

"Good." A pause, then, "Oops. Gotta go. He's coming back from the bathroom. See you later."

"Right. Bye." Still smiling, Julie slipped her cell phone into the front pocket of her jeans and opened the door. Instantly music slapped at her. Thundering drums, wailing guitars and the crash of the bass that jolted through the floorboards and up through the soles of her bare feet.

She shook her head, winced and headed down the dark hall. Sounds of the party drew her through the shadows into the kitchen. The lights were on, glancing off the bright yellow walls and white cabinets, searing into Julie's eyeballs like needles. On one side of the room, a man and woman were wrapped around each other as tightly as shrink wrap on a new DVD.

A quick jolt of envy shot through her, but Julie squashed it.

Sex=Bad.

If her hormones hadn't been doing the happy dance when she'd met Evan, none of this would have happened. Celibacy had to be better than letting your desires lead you down roads that only dead-ended.

Deliberately she turned her back on the couple, ignoring completely the muffled sighs and groans. But her insides twitched and a wash of heat ran through her despite all her efforts. To fight the neediness, she grabbed a spoon from the silverware drawer and headed for the one sensual delight that never let a woman down.

She yanked the freezer open and a chill blast of air wrapped itself around her. Snatching up the carton of ice cream, she took a moment to appreciate the fact that because she shared a house with a wannabe actress and a part-time model, the ice cream she bought was *always* in the freezer waiting for her. Smiling, Julie had the lid off and tossed onto the counter even before she swung the freezer door closed again.

"Whoa!" Startled, she took a step back and stared up into pale blue, icy eyes. "Didn't know you were there."

She hadn't even heard the man come into the room. Not a big surprise, though, considering the volume of the music. Although, she admitted silently, there was no way she could have missed this guy any other way. He shifted his cool gaze to the couple across the room from them and his jaw tightened.

Tall, at least six foot four, he had broad shoulders, long legs, night-black hair and sharply chiseled features. He was dressed all in black, from the jeans that hugged his legs to the T-shirt straining across a muscled chest to the three-quarter length coat that hung to the middle of his thighs.

A coat? In summer?

Ah, life in Hollywood, where image was everything.

When he swung those pale eyes back to her, Julie took a deep breath and a big bite of the ice cream. It wasn't enough to cool her off, though. She had a feeling that standing buck naked in a snowstorm wouldn't do it, either.

He frowned at her, then shook his head and glanced back to where the shrink-wrapped couple were practically horizontal on the counter. Before Julie could say anything, the tall, dark stranger was halfway across the room. He grabbed the guy's shoulder and spun him around.

Lover boy didn't much like the interruption. "Dude, what's your problem?"

"Hey," his girlfriend complained as she tugged her tube top back up to cover most of her breasts.

"Leave. Now."

Something in Mr. Tall, Dark and Dangerous's voice must have gotten through. The shorter man grabbed his girlfriend, swung her off the counter and tugged her across the room. Just before he slipped through the swinging door, though, he tossed back one last shot. "You are *so* lucky I don't feel like fighting tonight."

Julie half laughed as they disappeared into the main flow of the party. "You notice he didn't try to threaten you until he was sure he could escape."

"He's here. I know he's here. Somewhere."

"Who? Hell," Julie said, just a little nervous at being alone with a man bristling with a sense of power, "half of Hollywood's here tonight."

"This is your home." His gaze snapped to hers as his voice, deep and low, rumbled as insistently as the bass.

She swallowed. Everything about this man felt just a little over the top. Danger seemed to flash around him in electrical arcs that might as well have been lit by neon. He wasn't the ordinary guest who showed up to these parties. This man was...*different*. "Yeah. Why?"

He moved in closer and Julie felt heat rippling off of him in thick waves. Just watching him walk—long legs, slow, determined strides—was enough to make a woman go all hot and gooey. Not a man for a recently declared celibate to be around for very long. Her knees wobbled unsteadily even as her pulse kicked up into high gear.

It suddenly dawned on her that because of the noise level, if she had to yell for help, it wouldn't do any good. No one would hear her.

"Have you noticed any strangers here?"

"Huh? You mean besides you?" Julie forced another laugh and took a bigger bite of ice cream, still wildly hoping the frozen treat would cool off the heat building inside. "You're kidding, right?"

She waved her spoon at the closed swinging door separating the kitchen from the living room. "Everyone here is a stranger. Parties are free-for-alls in this town.

One person tells someone, who tells someone else who tells someone and—" she paused for yet another bite of ice cream "—you get the picture."

He scowled and his eyes narrowed. "That's what I thought."

Julie took another bite and momentarily savored the swirl of caramel as she studied him. Okay, maybe she wouldn't need help. What she'd need was a cold shower. Every cell in her body was tingling. Those eyes of his were downright hypnotic. She could almost feel herself leaning in toward him and it took everything she had to lean *back* instead.

His gaze swept the kitchen again, as if looking for something he'd missed in his first perusal. Finally, though, those eyes came back to her and she swallowed hard.

Still, he hadn't threatened her and she wasn't about to let him know she was even the slightest bit worried. She waved her empty spoon at him, sweeping up and down. "You're an actor, right?"

"No."

"Really?" Was it hot in the kitchen? Or was it just her body lighting up like a bonfire? "Because you've got the whole mysterious man of the night thing going and—"

"You should leave, too."

"Excuse me?"

"Leave," he repeated, reaching out to grab her upper arm. "Now."

His hand touched her bare arm and heat sizzled into life between them.

One of them definitely had a fever. She just wasn't sure which one.

He let her go almost instantly, and his eyes narrowed as he watched her. Like he was blaming *her* for that short burst of fire.

Stepping back from him, Julie said, "It's one thing for you to throw Don Juan and the bimbo out, but this is my house." At least one third of it. And right about now, she'd be really happy to see either Alicia or Kate come marching through that door. The kitchen seemed to be getting smaller. And hotter. "I'm not going anywhere. But I think you should."

Kieran MacIntyre felt the fire still burning his fingertips and a part of him stood back and wondered at it. Through the countless centuries he'd been wandering this earth, he'd never experienced that jolt. He'd known others of his kind who had and, in the beginning, he'd even been jealous of it.

But as time passed and the years piled up behind him like dirty beads on a piece of string, he'd learned that he was the lucky one. He had no distractions to keep him from the hunt. He had no other to worry about. He didn't have to concern himself with agonizing over the loss of a Mate when he'd never found one.

Until now.

He'd first become aware of her three months ago when she'd called his home trying to set up an interview with him. Naturally her request was rejected, but he'd looked her up online and had been immediately intrigued. Her photo had haunted him since and he'd made it his business to keep a distant eye on her. Until tonight of course, when he'd been forced to confront her.

Stray curls of dark red hair escaped from the ridiculous ponytail she wore at the top of her head. Her green eyes were huge in a pale face sprinkled with just a few golden freckles. Instinct pushed at him to grab her. Hold her. Tip her head back, taste her neck, feel her pulse pound beneath his mouth. Fill his hands with her breasts and bury himself in her heat.

His body roared with life and a hunger he'd never known before. And he didn't want it. Didn't need it. He'd survived for this long without a Mate and he'd done a hell of a job of it, too. He'd never liked complications. Not in life and certainly not since his death. Easier by far to keep his distance from the mortal world, do his job and then fade from the memory of everyone whose life he'd touched.

Better to be alone.

Count on no one but himself and the other Guardians.

But she smelled sweet. Fresh.

Alive.

The floral shampoo she used clung to her seductively and he wondered if her skin would taste as good as she smelled. Her high, full breasts rose and fell quickly with her agitated breathing and her eyes seemed to get bigger, wider, as she watched him.

Did she sense the connection between them?

Could she have any idea at all about what was to come?

"Who are you?" she asked quietly, her whisper almost swallowed by the noise drifting to them from the adjacent room.

Who was he? An interesting question. Guardian? Warrior? Knight? Too many answers and not enough time.

He took a step closer, and she moved, too, backing up until she bumped into the kitchen counter behind her. She jolted in surprise and dropped the carton of ice cream to the floor.

She couldn't know. Couldn't even imagine the world he moved through.

His gaze locked with hers, Kieran moved in even closer, dipping his head, letting her fill him with scents that drugged him, that poured through him like rich wine.

His heartbeat thundered in his chest.

He had no time for this. And yet, he knew he couldn't leave her without one taste. Since he first saw her photo, he'd known this moment would come—now, he wouldn't waste it. Cupping her cheeks between his palms, he took her mouth, intending only a brief, hard kiss that would assuage the sudden, all-encompassing need raging within. But one brush of her lips to his and he was lost.

She sighed into his mouth and her lips opened for

him. His tongue swept into her depths and he felt himself drowning in the heat of her. Senses overloading, his body felt engulfed in flames. She sighed again and the soft sound spiraled through him like knives, tearing through a centuries old apathy as if it were fragile silk.

Her breasts pressed to his chest, he felt the thundering beat of her heart as if it were his own. It shuddered through him, pounding in his head, his blood.

She dropped the spoon and it clattered on the tile floor like a warning bell.

Kieran groaned, let her go and reluctantly stepped away, willing his body into quiet. The instinct to take her was strong, nearly overpowering. She trembled, eyes wide, and he wanted to lay her down on the floor and lose himself in the heat of her.

"Wow," she said softly, "you're really good at that."

He rubbed one hand across his mouth and refused to admit he was shaking. He had no time for this. No time to be distracted by something he wasn't going to claim anyway.

He wasn't here for her.

Exactly.

Kieran had followed the scent of his prey to this house. All day, he'd hunted it, always a step or two behind. Tracking the elusive trace energy signature all demons left in their wake. Now, it seemed that Fate had taken a turn in the hunt. Why else would the beast he sought have come here?

To *her* house?

The power of the beast throbbed in the air, its hunger, its desire pulsing wildly and it amazed Kieran anew that the mortals couldn't sense it. Somewhere in this house, the demon moved freely, already on the hunt, deciding who it would kill and when.

And he was the only man who could stop it.

* * * * *

Don't miss the exciting conclusion to
Maureen Child's ETERNALLY
from her GUARDIANS *miniseries.*
When you accept our offer for 2 free books
you will receive a copy of ETERNALLY *free*.*
Please look inside your envelope or call
Customer Service for details.

*while supplies last.

Get 2 free books when you subscribe to Silhouette® Nocturne™.

nocturne™

Save $1.⁰⁰ off

your purchase of any Silhouette Nocturne novel at your favorite retailer!

Receive $1.00 off
any Silhouette Nocturne novel

Available wherever books are sold, including most bookstores, supermarkets, drug stores and discount stores.

Coupon expires May 31, 2007. Redeemable at participating retail outlets in the U.S. only. Limit one coupon per customer.

5 65373 00076 2   (8100) 0 11304

SNCUSDTC

nocturne™

Save $1.^{00} off

your purchase of any Silhouette Nocturne novel at your favorite retailer!